For Marcus

Published in 2011 by Simply Read Books
www.simplyreadbooks.com

Text and illustrations © 2011 Michael Moniz

Library and Archives Canada Cataloguing in Publication

Moniz, Michael
Wazzyjump / written and illustrated by Michael Moniz.

ISBN 978-1-897476-58-1

Title.

PS8626.O54W39   2011   jC813'.6   C2011-900171-3

We gratefully acknowledge for their financial support of our publishing program the Canada Council
for the Arts, the BC Arts Council, and the Government of Canada through the Canada Book Fund (CBF).

Manufactured by C&C, Offset in China, July 2011
This product conforms to CPSIA 2008

Book design by Michael Moniz and Natasha Kanji

10 9 8 7 6 5 4 3 2 1

Wazzyjump

By Michael Moniz

SIMPLY READ BOOKS

A long time ago, in a
big wooded forest not so far away,
there lived a little brown rabbit
named Wazzyjump.

𝓘t was rumored that Wazzyjump was a magical creature. Some
animals thought he could run impossibly fast.

Others thought he could disappear at will. But no one really knew what powers he possessed.

$\mathcal{W}$azzyjump was also the most mysterious of the forest creatures. The other animals had only ever caught a glimpse of him from behind as he darted through the woods.

When the ruler of all the beasts, a great lion, visited the forest he heard tales of Wazzyjump. Lion could not stand the thought that any creature was more special than he. He vowed to capture Wazzyjump so he could take the creature's magic for himself, no matter what it was.

$\mathcal{L}$ion summoned all the creatures from the bumbling bee to the burly bear. "Search the forest," he ordered. "Find Wazzyjump and bring him to me."

The winged creatures searched from above.

While the sure-footed creatures searched below.

Even Bear, in his own lazy way, searched for Wazzyjump. But neither he, nor any of the other animals, could find him.

Little did they know that deep in the hollow of an old tree, Wazzyjump hid and slept safe and snug. Eventually, all of the animals gave up their search, except for one.

Fox was not like the others. He was mischievous, clever and very patient. And he was also not impressed with the visiting lion. "Why should I give the magic to Lion?" thought Fox. "If I find Wazzyjump—which I surely will—I'll keep his magic for myself."

Fox studied Wazzyjump's trail. Slowly, he began tracking the paw prints, here and there, all over the forest.

Until eventually, he stood in front of the unsuspecting, sleeping Wazzyjump. He approached Wazzyjump with great stealth.

"At last," he whispered. "I found you."

At the sound of Fox's voice, Wazzyjump awoke. Fox pounced.

$\mathscr{W}$azzyjump dodged … Frustrated, Fox flung himself at Wazzyjump. But Wazzyjump dodged again … and this time Wazzyjump laughed.

$\mathcal{B}$efore Fox knew it, he was laughing too. Then they both began to play. They laughed and played all afternoon.

From then on, everyday, Fox trotted to Wazzyjump's hollow tree to play. He forgot all about Wazzyjump's magic.

One morning, on his way to Wazzyjump, Fox bumped into Bear.

"Where are you going in such a hurry?" asked Bear.

Fox just scampered on.

"*That's* strange," thought Bear, as he watched Fox rush away. "I wonder what he's up to."

Curious, the usually lazy bear bounded up and followed Fox. When he reached the hollow tree, he couldn't believe his eyes. Wazzyjump! Fox was playing with Wazzyjump!

"Should I tell Lion?" he wondered, then decided, "I'll ask my friend Raccoon what to do."

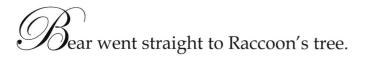ear went straight to Raccoon's tree.

"Raccoon! Raccoon! I saw Fox playing with Wazzyjump. What should we do?"

Raccoon twitched his tail. "Wow! I don't know. I'll ask my friend, Jay!"

Raccoon hurried and scurried to Jay's tree. "Jay! Jay! Bear saw Fox playing with Wazzyjump! What should he do?"

Jay flapped his wings in excitement. "Wow! I'm not sure. I'll ask my friends, the other birds."

$\mathcal{J}$ay, flapping and fluttering, chirped the news all over the forest.

"Fox found Wazzyjump! They're playing by the hollow tree!"

$\mathcal{S}$oon the story of Fox and Wazzyjump reached the ears of the great Lion. "Fox found Wazzyjump and didn't tell me? How dare he!" roared Lion.

$\mathcal{L}$ion ran to the hollow tree as fast as his massive paws could carry him, desperate to catch Wazzyjump, capture his magic and punish Fox.

Bear trembled for the safety of poor Fox. He felt terrible for getting Fox in trouble.

At last, Lion, seething, reached Fox and Wazzyjump.

*H*e leapt at them from out of the bushes. "You stole the magic meant for me!" he bellowed.

Fox cowered and trembled. "I didn't steal anything," he cried.

Lion roared in rage. He pounced and missed. Pounced and missed. Again and again he pounced, and again and again Fox and Wazzyjump dodged away. Wazzyjump started to laugh. Fox couldn't help but laugh too. Lion was so enraged …

He sat on the ground with a thump. He was so frustrated, so powerless, he was beyond roaring. There was only one thing left to do …

He laughed. Quickly, Lion's laugh grew from a rumble to a happy roar.

" Come play with us some more," said Fox and Wazzyjump. And to Bear, who was watching all the while, they added, "Come join us too." Soon all four of them began to play and laugh together.

$\mathcal{L}$ater, taking a rest, Lion asked, "What exactly is your magic, little rabbit?"

"What magic?" laughed Wazzyjump, hopping up to play some more.

Could it be Wazzyjump wasn't magical at all? Lion, Fox and Bear simply shrugged and joined their friend.

*N*ow when you visit the forest, if you listen very carefully, you might hear the laughter of the friends at play — Lion, Fox, Bear … and, of course, Wazzyjump.

The End

CONTENTS

World Religions: By the Numbers

According to a 2017 Pew Research Center demographic analysis, Christians were the largest religious group in the world in 2015. However, that may be changing. The same analysis projects Muslims to be the world's fastest-growing major religious group over the next four decades.

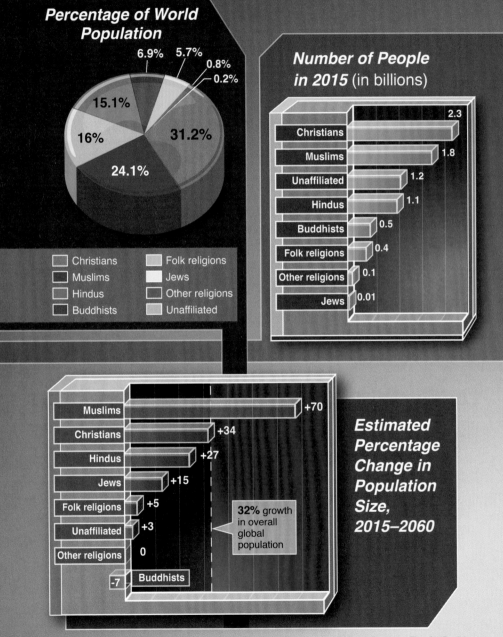

Percentage of World Population

- 6.9%
- 5.7%
- 0.8%
- 0.2%
- 15.1%
- 16%
- 31.2%
- 24.1%

Legend:
- Christians
- Muslims
- Hindus
- Buddhists
- Folk religions
- Jews
- Other religions
- Unaffiliated

Number of People in 2015 (in billions)

Religion	Billions
Christians	2.3
Muslims	1.8
Unaffiliated	1.2
Hindus	1.1
Buddhists	0.5
Folk religions	0.4
Other religions	0.1
Jews	0.01

Estimated Percentage Change in Population Size, 2015–2060

Religion	Change
Muslims	+70
Christians	+34
Hindus	+27
Jews	+15
Folk religions	+5
Unaffiliated	+3
Other religions	0
Buddhists	-7

32% growth in overall global population

Source: Conrad Hackett and David McClendon, "Christians Remain World's Largest Religious Group, but They Are Declining in Europe," Pew Research Center: The Changing Global Religious Landscape, April 5, 2017. www.pewresearch.org.

The Power of Good Deeds

The Indian religious figure Swami Vivekananda—whose birth name was Narendranath—was born in 1863, and by the time of his passing in 1902 he had become widely venerated among Hindus everywhere. *Swami* was not his first name but rather his title. In Sanskrit, the ancient language used to record classic Indian and Hindu literature, *swami* translates literally as "one who is at one with his inner self." The term denotes a monk who has found inner peace through prayer and other spiritual means. In Hindu society, a swami, whom many Hindus also call a yogi, is generally viewed as unusually wise and is therefore highly respected.

Today some expert observers call Swami Vivekananda a pivotal religious activist because he steadfastly promoted the Hindu faith throughout his adult life. In particular, he gained fame for giving pro-Hindu speeches in numerous foreign countries, including the United States. Those who attended the lectures learned that Hinduism was the world's third-largest religion, after Christianity and Islam. In 2018, more than a century after the swami's death, Hinduism remains in third place, with some 1.2 billion believers.

Baba and the Thief

Besides teaching groups of non-Hindus about his faith, Swami Vivekananda also frequently dealt with ordinary people one on one. In each instance, he tried to teach a moral, social, or spiritual lesson. In one of his better-known personal interactions, the swami traveled to Rishikesh, a small city located in the foothills of the lofty Himalayas in northern India. There, by chance, he met a fellow monk, who greeted him with a bow of the head to indicate his respect. The swami returned the gesture and the two men walked together for a while through a local park. After that, they swiftly became good friends.

One day the monk, who was well-known and hugely respected in the region, asked, "Dear Swami, have you heard of Pavhari Baba?" The swami replied, "Yes, I have heard of him," and described Baba as a great sage, or exceptionally wise person. The monk went on, "Then have you heard of the story of a thief who tried to steal from Pavhari Baba?"[1]

Eagerly, the monk told the story of how a young Indian man, who had turned to thievery as a way of life, had been keeping a close watch on Baba's house for several days. The thief noticed that Baba often came and went carrying silver candlesticks and other valuable artifacts. Eventually, the young man snuck into the house and started loading the silver items into a cloth bag. All of a sudden, Baba appeared; the thief was so startled that he dropped the bag and ran. A while later, noticing that Baba was in hot pursuit, the young man increased his speed, but in time he became exhausted and collapsed on the ground. Baba caught up and stood over the thief.

At that point the sage could have had the thief arrested and testified against him in court. In that case, the young man would have been convicted and spent two or three years in jail. But to the thief's surprise, that was not what Baba did. Instead, the sage produced the bag of silver artifacts the thief had left behind and said, "All these are yours. Please take them all."[2] Having freely given the perpetrator the very goods he had sought to steal, Baba turned and walked away.

A Jewel of Wisdom

After he had told Swami Vivekananda the story, the monk said that he had something important to add: "I was that thief!"[3] The swami realized what had happened. Instead of reporting the thief to the police, Baba had shown him mercy and kindness. Overcome and greatly inspired by the gesture, the young man had turned his life around and eventually became a spiritual person and a valued member of society.

In later years, Swami Vivekananda retold the story of Baba and the thief many times. It proved to be a potent example of

Hindus believe that the best way to create and spread goodness in society is to treat others as they would themselves want to be treated. This is a guiding principle of Hinduism, as practiced by young Hindus in India (pictured) and around the world.

how good deeds like Baba's have the potential power to change both one person's life and society as a whole for the better. The swami told people how this principle is one of the main pillars of Hinduism. Indeed, he said, classic Hindu religious texts teach that practicing good deeds tends to produce more good behavior by oneself and others over the course of time. In contrast, if people regularly perform selfish or bad deeds, it has negative effects on those individuals, as well as on their community.

Building on these concepts, the swami explained the major Hindu belief that the most common way to create and perpetuate goodness in society is to treat others as they themselves would like to be treated. That jewel of wisdom is one of many in the great Hindu epic known as the Mahabharata. "This is the sum of duty," it states. "Do not do to others what would cause pain if done to you."[4]

This old adage is very familiar to most people in Western societies, including American culture, where it is known as the Golden Rule. Christians know it best in the form it takes in the Gospel of Matthew: "In everything, do to others as you would have them do to you."[5] Those words are attributed to Jesus in his Sermon on the Mount. Yet the concept of the adage was not original to him since the Mahabharata predated him by many centuries. In fact, the Golden Rule is universal—found in the writings of dozens of peoples of all faiths throughout most of recorded history.

> "Do not do to others what would cause pain if done to you."[4]
>
> —The Mahabharata

As it turns out, Hinduism—the earliest major religion to appear—was the first large-scale faith to adopt that concept. Moreover, as Swami Vivekananda pointed out many times, Hindus elevated that idea of the power of righteous actions to a central position in their faith. There, to this day, it continues to change countless lives for the better.

CHAPTER ONE

The Origins of Hinduism

University of Wales comparative religion scholar Gavin Flood was asked on numerous occasions to explain the origins and meaning of the term *Hindu*. So when he wrote his long, thoughtful introduction to the great world religion known as Hinduism, he said,

> The actual term "hindu" first occurs as a Persian geographical term for the people who lived beyond the river Indus. In Arabic texts, Al-Hind is a term for the people of modern-day India, and "Hindu" or "Hindoo," was used toward the end of the nineteenth century by the British to refer to the people of "Hindustan," the area of northwest India. Eventually, "Hindu" became virtually equivalent to an Indian who was not a Muslim, Sikh, Jain, or Christian, thereby encompassing a range of religious beliefs and practices.[6]

Clearly, then, *India*, *Hindu*, and *Hinduism* are all early modern terms imposed on India's residents by outsiders. Historically, Indians called their land Bharata-varsha. Also, the ancient term for what is now the Hindu faith, or Hinduism, was *Sanatana-dharma*.

One reason why non-Indians came to coin the Indian and Hindu terms in wide use today was due to the outsiders' genuine confusion. The Persians, Greeks, British, and others who invaded India one by one over the centuries were awed and bewildered by that land's enormous size. They were equally mystified by the fantastic cultural diversity of the locals and their religious beliefs. Indeed, the outsiders discovered that dozens of different faiths had developed in India during ancient and medieval times, and three of them—today known as Hinduism, Buddhism, and Jainism—eventually attracted so many followers that they came to be ranked among the ten largest world religions.

Of all those local Indian faiths, Hinduism was the earliest to develop, had the biggest following, and was by far structurally the most complex. "One reason for the complexity of Hinduism," scholar Karel Werner explains,

> is the fact that it has no known starting point and no single charismatic [inspiring] figure who could be regarded as its originator. It took shape over a period of many hundreds of years and many diverse influences left their mark on its fabric. It is therefore by following, at least in brief outline, the historical sequences and developments in the religious scene which led to the emergence of Hinduism as a religious system that we can hope to start appreciating its many facets and the way they form a multifarious [diverse] yet coherent whole.[7]

The Harappan-Vedic Connection

Those "historical sequences" that led to the emergence of Hinduism began long ago and are largely shrouded in the hazy mists of the dim past. Modern historians think that during the mid-second millennium BCE (about thirty-five hundred years ago), a culture known today as Vedic emerged in northern India, and that the gods and other elements of the Vedic people's religion were destined over time to lay the foundations of what would eventually be called Hinduism. In other words, Hinduism is a latter-day, mature, and more complex version of the original Vedic faith.

Exactly who the Vedic people were and where they came from are still somewhat unclear. But most modern experts now lean toward the idea that they developed from an earlier Indian culture that is called both the Harappan culture and the Indus Valley civilization. It is possible, then, that some primitive elements of Hinduism originated with the Harappans.

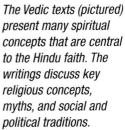

The Vedic texts (pictured) present many spiritual concepts that are central to the Hindu faith. The writings discuss key religious concepts, myths, and social and political traditions.

Some surviving evidence suggests that Hinduism's roots do stretch back to the Harappan culture. In particular, archaeologists have dug up more than thirty-five hundred carvings done on seals—small objects, most often made of stone, that people used to make impressions in soft clay. The artisans then put the clay out in the sun to dry or baked it in a kiln, resulting in hard, long-lasting artifacts that they used as their written records since they did not have paper. Those who used seals to make the initial impressions in the clay were most often members of the upper classes who wanted to stamp their authority on contracts, decrees, and other permanent records. Artisans and merchants also used seals to make personalized marks that established their creation or ownership of various goods.

Several of these seals bear carved images that suggest that those who made them held at least some beliefs similar to those of both the Vedic faith and Hinduism. One seal, for instance, bears an image that may represent Murugan, a Hindu war god. This implies that Hinduism's roots may be very ancient indeed. Scholar of Indian mythology Devdutt Pattanaik writes that "there is increasing evidence that by the time Vedic civilisation established itself in [northern India], it was influenced by Harappan ideas and practices."[8]

Vedic Religious Writings

Whatever the connections between Harappan and Vedic religions may have been, there is no doubt that the Vedic faith produced numerous spiritual concepts that later became central elements of Hinduism. Vedic writers created some imposing literary works that in time came to underpin Hinduism as well as the Vedic faith. These writings provide an informative overview of Vedic religious concepts, myths about the Vedic gods, and a number of social and political traditions. Of those Vedic literary works that survive, the most important and celebrated are the Vedas. Their specific authors remain unknown, but the strong religious themes that run through them suggest that at least some of them were Brahmans, members of the powerful class of priests.

The oldest and probably best known of the Vedas is the *Rig-Veda* (which translates literally as "rich in knowledge"). It comprises ten subsections, usually referred to as books, each of which contains several hymns to a diverse collection of Vedic gods. Three other Vedas—the *Sama-Veda*, *Yajur-Veda*, and *Atharva-Veda*, also containing hymns—appeared somewhat later than the *Rig-Veda*.

The numerous hymns in the Vedas tell a great deal about the Vedic gods and the religious system employed in India during the Vedic age (ca. 1500–500 BCE). Many of the deities mentioned in the hymns, who later became Hindu gods, were seen as related to natural forces such as wind, fire, storms, earth-quakes, the sun, the changing sky, and so forth. Some gods are mentioned considerably more often than the others in the hymns. One—Indra, with 250 hymns dedicated to him—was the leading Vedic deity.

A Grand Spiritual Evolution

Worship of Indra and the other Vedic gods did not take place in temples; these specialized structures emerged later in India. Rather, worshippers built hearth-like altars outdoors. On them they enacted the primary ritual of their faith: fire sacrifices dedicated to the fire god, Agni. Brahman priests oversaw the ceremonies, in which people lit sacred fires and chanted hymns, including many immortalized in writing in the Vedas. This aspect of worship later became central to Hinduism. According to one expert, Hindus see fire as "both the creator and destroyer of life, and those that follow the Hindu tradition recognize this fact through several of their rituals and practices. Fire plays a role in cremations, the worship of important deities through sacrifices and offerings and in daily Hindu routines."[9]

In this way, the Vedic faith, which appears somehow to have evolved from the more ancient and mysterious Harappan religion, established a sort of groundwork for Hinduism. In this respect, then, Hinduism had no known specific founders, nor any tangible dates for the introduction of specific Hindu beliefs and practices over the centuries. Instead, classical, or full-fledged and mature, Hinduism simply replaced, or overwrote, the Vedic faith over time. Exactly how much time was involved is still not precisely known. Hinduism developed in fits and starts, a little at a time, throughout the classical period (ca. 500 BCE–ca. 500 CE) and even well into the faith's medieval period (ca. 500 CE–ca. 1500 CE).

During these eras both religious literature and the fine arts played essential roles in evolving Hinduism into its mature form. Especially important among those artistic expressions that helped to shape the faith were sculptures and paintings of the gods that Hindus came to worship regularly. The beliefs and rituals associated with those deities developed directly out of Vedic traditions.

Indra Slays the Dragon

As the leading Vedic god, Indra not only had numerous hymns dedicated to him but also played a central role in several important myths. The similarity between some of these stories and versions that developed in Greece and other parts of Europe may be coincidental, but many historians suspect that some sort of cultural diffusion—or periodic, informal interchange of ideas and tales—occurred among these ancient civilizations. According to the renowned scholar of Vedic culture Karel Werner, the most important of Indra's myths

> describes creation as the combat with the serpent-demon or dragon Vrtra, whom he pierced with his spear, thereby releasing waters, or rescuing captive maidens, symbolizing the powers of creation. [This is similar to] the Greek myths of Perseus and Andromeda and of Theseus and Ariadne, and tales from European folklore about the knight in shining armor rescuing a princess from a dragon, and the legend of St. George [slaying a dragon]. In another creation myth Indra is described as separating heaven and earth and propping them up with his spear to keep them apart. [On] the popular level in later Hinduism Indra is mostly regarded as the rain god [and is] seen, in this context, as killing the demon Vrtra, who is here represented by monsoon clouds, with his spear (lightning), thereby releasing the life-giving waters.

Karel Werner, *A Popular Dictionary of Hinduism*. Chicago: NTC, 1997, p. 79.

In some cases, the divine beings in question underwent noticeable changes during the transition from the older faith to the newer one. A clear example is the chief Vedic god, Indra. To Vedic worshippers he was a very powerful war god who also had charge of rain, storms, thunder, lightning, and other weather phenomena. To later Hindu worshippers, however, Indra was a lesser weather god whose reputation was marred by his periodic bouts with alcoholism. Much more powerful and respected in the Hindu pantheon (group of gods) were Brahma, called "the Creator"; Vishnu, known as "the Preserver"; and Shiva, who bore the fearsome title of "the Destroyer." Hindus came to view those three deities as part of a trilogy, or trinity, in some ways similar to the Christian Holy Trinity of Father, Son, and Holy Ghost.

Hindus call that sacred grouping the Trimurti. True to his nickname, Hindus say, the first member of the Trimurti, Brahma, created the earth and heavens. Meanwhile, one expert observer writes, "Vishnu preserves and protects the universe and has appeared on the earth through his avatars (incarnations) to save humankind from natural disasters or from tyranny."[10] In contrast, as official cosmic destroyer, Shiva oversees the elimination of old, outdated aspects of the world, including human nations and various natural landforms.

Mature Hinduism also features a number of other Vedic gods who serve diverse functions within the natural order. Among the better-known examples are Ganesh (or Ganesha), deity of wisdom, who has the head of an elephant; Mitra, who oversees friendships and the concept of truth; the fire god, Agni; Varuna, lord of the seas and lakes; and the sun god, Surya. Particularly admired by all Hindus is Hanuman, who has a man's body and a monkey's face. He is known for his physical strength and heroism in fighting for righteous causes, and one of the more popular hymns sung to him prays, "Lord Hanuman, give me strength, intelligence, and knowledge, [and] cure my body ailments and mental imperfections."[11]

Key Literary Works

In the same way that Hinduism incorporated some of the Vedic gods into its own pantheon, several key literary works were transferred from the Vedic religion into the Hindu faith. Particularly crucial were ancient India's two magnificent epic poems: the Ramayana and the Mahabharata. Some idea of how important they were, and still are, to all Hindus can be seen in what happened when the tales told in the Ramayana were dramatized for the first time in a long television miniseries during the early 1990s. On Sunday mornings, when the episodes were broadcast, the streets of India's cities were almost deserted because most people were indoors glued to their televisions. Meanwhile, stores that carried televisions quickly sold out of them, and people who could not afford one of their own went to relatives' or neighbors' houses to see the show. Also, in many cities the buses stopped running because the drivers stayed home to watch.

The Ramayana tells the story of how the wondrous preserver god, Vishnu, awakens from a long, refreshing sleep to find the disturbing news that the appalling demon king, Ravana, is corrupting human society. To stop the monster, Vishnu goes to Earth as one of his many avatars. In this case he is born into an Indian royal family as a prince named Rama. As he grows into an adult, Rama becomes involved in various adventures and intrigues before finally slaying the evil Ravana and thereby saving humanity.

At around fifteen times the length of the Bible, the other great Hindu epic—the Mahabharata—is even longer than the Ramayana as well as more involved and intricate. As Finnish scholar Jukka O. Miettinen explains,

> The Mahabharata could be regarded as the national epic of India. It is the world's largest epic poem, consisting of some 100,000 double verses. Like other great epics, the Mahabharata, written in Sanskrit, is a collective work, and its author is unknown. It has been generally assumed that

Statues of the elephant-headed god Ganesh can be seen at this Hindu temple in Malaysia. The elephant's large head is a symbol of wisdom; its oversize ears represent the ability to listen to many different opinions.

the poem relates events that happened during a period of tribal warfare in Northern India in approximately the ninth century BCE. [The] Mahabharata gradually became a cornerstone of Hindu thinking. In its richness and diversity of levels, [it] is not only an ageless description of ancient clan disputes and bloody warfare, but also an image of an ultimately Indian and Hindu way of conceiving the world and man's duty in it.[12]

Both of the great Hindu epics contain numerous passages in which characters—most often Vishnu or another deity in an earthly guise—explain important Hindu beliefs or concepts. A typical example occurs in the sacred Bhagavad Gita, a subsection of the larger Mahabharata. Here, Krishna, one of Vishnu's human incarnations, urges a group of soldiers to enter battle without fear. They need not dread dying, he says, because their souls will be reincarnated. There will never "be a time when we shall not exist," Krishna tells them. Indeed, he says,

> *"It is said of the indestructible, infinite soul that it is eternal."*[13]
>
> —Vishnu's avatar Krishna in the Bhagavad Gita

we all exist from now on. As the soul experiences in this body childhood, youth, and old age, so also it acquires another body. . . . Know that indestructible essence by which all this is pervaded. No one is able to cause the destruction of the imperishable [soul]. These bodies have an end; it is said of the indestructible, infinite soul that it is eternal.[13]

A Dense Pictorial Encyclopedia

Like key works of religious literature, the production of art and architecture that can expressly be called Hindu in inspiration and form strongly affected the emerging Hindu faith. In part, these visual arts provided the new religion with a recognizable identity. They emphasized and helped to signify that certain traditional rituals, hymns, and beliefs were Hindu—not Vedic nor Buddhist

A Connection Between Humans and the Divine

The late Harvard University scholar Benjamin Rowland, an international authority on ancient Indian art, explains that early Hindu art was a reflection of ancient Indian art as a whole. In large part, he says, it was bound up with a person's desire to develop a meaningful connection with the divine forces that shaped the world around him or her. Rowland makes this concept clearer with an analogy involving simple numbers:

> The Indian view of life and religion could be said to be based upon the idea that the ordinary world which we see around us is the only aspect of the infinite deity known to us. In Indian art the world is regarded as an appearance of God. This can in a measure explain the seemingly "realistic" portrayal of many forms of nature in all periods of Indian art. The divine is thought of as present in humans and in nature, present in the same way that the number one is present, though invisible, within [the numbers] two, three, four, and five. ... It is the aim of all the Indian religions—Hindu, Buddhist, and Jain—to [try] to know the divinity directly.

Benjamin Rowland, *The Art and Architecture of India.* New York: Penguin, 1977, p. 8.

nor Jain nor anything else but authentic Hindu. Indeed, the establishment of authentic Hindu arts gave the developing faith validity and legitimacy in the eyes of the many non-Hindus in India and the rest of southern Asia.

At the same time, the emergence of identifiable, often magnificently crafted Hindu arts reassured worshippers—in a way, proving to them that their belief system was both real and worthy. The website of the University of Missouri Museum of Art and Archaeology explains:

> From its beginnings Hindu art was created primarily to aid devotees in focusing their worship. Monumental stone statues or relief sculptures were positioned in or on temples, and large bronze cult statues were set up for public worship.

Innumerable smaller figurines have been made for installation in household shrines so that devotees may offer personal devotion. Paintings, tapestries, ritual objects, theatrical masks, and other items bearing images of deities have been created in various media, all forming part of a dense pictorial encyclopedia used to illustrate divine subject matter. This rich corpus of imagery provides instruction, support, and inspiration for millions of devout Hindu believers.[14]

Hindu art has long displayed potent examples of symbolism, the artistic device or style in which one image stands for or enhances the power of a certain idea or physical reality. A familiar example is the frequent depiction of gods and other supernatural beings with multiple arms or even multiple heads. Non-Hindus often assume that the artist is being literal and that a deity shown with four arms is thought by Hindus to actually possess four arms. In reality, however, these are examples of artistic symbolism and are not meant to be taken literally. Columbia University scholar Vidya Dehejia explains that in Hindu art,

> *"The multiplicity of arms emphasizes the immense power of the deity."*[15]
>
> —Columbia University scholar Vidya Dehejia

deities are frequently portrayed with multiple arms, especially when they are engaged in combative acts of cosmic consequence that involve destroying powerful forces of evil. The multiplicity of arms emphasizes the immense power of the deity and his or her ability to perform several feats at the same time. The Indian artist found this a simple and an effective means of expressing the omnipresence and omnipotence of a deity.[15]

A more detailed example of symbolism in Hindu art is the common depiction of the elephant-headed god, Ganesh. Hindu artists did not choose to give him elephant-like traits because he was thought to actually look like that animal. Rather, the average

Hindu understands that the deity's real form is unknowable by humans. But for the sake of convenience and artistic license, elephantine characteristics were chosen to emphasize certain qualities that the god was thought to possess.

For example, in ancient India people saw an elephant's large head as a sign of wisdom and understanding. Similarly, the creature's oversize ears were seen to symbolize an ability to listen to others' opinions. These and other aspects of elephant anatomy were used in sculptures and paintings to show that Ganesh was wise, a good listener, compassionate, and strong enough to face life's many difficulties. Scholar Marilyn McFarlane adds that in Hindu artistic renditions of the god,

> there is usually a rat (sometimes a mouse or shrew) under the god's feet. The rodent represents the ego, which sits beneath him because control of the ego is necessary for spiritual growth. It is also a reminder that just as rodents can gnaw through almost any wall, so Ganesh can overcome any obstacle. As an elephant he can pass through thick forest, and by riding on a small animal he can pass through a tiny opening.[16]

An Air of Authenticity and Importance

The most visually complete and detailed examples of Indian art were the temples erected across India beginning in the fourth century CE. These superbly crafted edifices were instrumental in stimulating the final stages of mature Hinduism's formation because they gave the faith a public identity. In earlier ages families had worshipped either in their homes or at small altars they had set up in nearby fields or the closest caves. The presence of large, impressively decorated structures dedicated to Hindu worship gave the faith a strong sense of wider communal spirit. In fact, researcher Mark Cartwright explains, "Temples inevitably became the very center of a community and, accordingly, their upkeep was guaranteed by land grants and endowments from the ruling class, as indicated by inscriptions on many temples."[17]

Ornate temples such as this one in southern India provide a place for believers to find inspiration and a sense of the Hindu faith's communal spirit. Large, highly decorated temples can be found throughout India.

People could and did continue to worship at home, but they now added periodic visits to temples that visually defined what it meant to be a Hindu. Those visual elements also provide worshippers with vital information about their faith; sculptured figures on and in Hindu temples remind the faithful about episodes from the adventures of Vishnu and other Hindu gods.

Like other examples of Hindu arts, as well as Hindu sacred literature, Hindu architecture provided the faith with its own recognizable themes and qualities, endowing it with an air of authenticity and importance. By the end of the first millennium CE, hundreds of ornate temples dotted India's landscape. These edifices, along with other forms of artistic expression, and the faith's already well-established sacred writings and worship rituals, had by that time all combined into a complex and imposing religious system. Hinduism had reached a fully developed, mature form. Hindu artists, poets, and philosophers would continue polishing and honing the faith's existing structure in the centuries to come. But the broad outlines of a great world religion, whose roots stretched back dozens of centuries into humanity's past, were solidly in place.

CHAPTER TWO

What Do Hindus Believe?

Deeply imbedded in the Hindu belief system, and wonderfully illustrated by all aspects of Hindu art, is a wide array of gods and goddesses. Some were borrowed directly from the earlier Vedic faith, but others were adopted through the centuries from regional Indian cultures. As a whole, the Hindu gods are so numerous and depicted so often in the arts that their presence is usually the first aspect of the faith that outsiders see when they visit India. In the words of Lancaster University scholar Kim Knott,

> Hindu gods and goddesses are everywhere in India, hidden within gorgeous temples and small wayside shrines, depicted in intricate stone carvings, looking out benevolently from advertisements, calendar prints, and film posters, and captured on market stalls and in shop windows in jewelry and small sculptures. They are woven into the fabric of life in Indian villages and cities, and are now also to be found in Hindu communities from the Caribbean to North America and Europe, from South Africa to Thailand. They are much loved by all. The many places in which they appear and the multitude of forms they take indicate the diversity and richness of Hindu culture.[18]

Making God More Relatable

A majority of those non-Hindu visitors to India tend to assume that Hinduism is polytheistic, or characterized by the worship of multiple distinct gods. However, Hinduism is, beneath its outward display of multiple gods, monotheistic like Christianity, Judaism, and Islam. The early Hindus kept most of the Vedic gods and even added several more, yet at the same time they added a very important new concept all their own.

That idea—then highly unusual in the ancient world—was that a divine being named Brahman (not to be confused with Brahma, one of the three deities in the Trimurti) was the one and only real god. A majority of ancient Hindus came to view Brahman as a dominant, paramount, universal spirit, which they called the Ishvara. A modern Hindu monk describes that sole divinity, saying,

> God is unmanifest [imperceptible], unchanging, and transcendent [beyond all], the Self God, timeless, formless and spaceless. As Pure Consciousness, God is the manifest primal substance, pure love and light flowing through all form, existing everywhere in time and space as infinite intelligence and power. As Primal Soul, God is our personal Lord, source of all three worlds, our Father-Mother God who protects, nurtures and guides us. We beseech God's grace in our lives while also knowing that He/She is the essence of our soul, the life of our life.[19]

Considering that Hindus believe there is only one actual all-powerful god, it is only natural to wonder why they worship all those other diverse deities. The primary reason is that those extra gods are not separate entities, each unto itself; rather, they are various manifestations, guises, or aspects of the single true god. The belief is that Brahman exists on a heavenly, or spiritual, level far beyond Earth and other material parts of the universe. Meanwhile, humans view and worship Brahman in varying ways, mostly according to local customs established long ago.

One way of looking at this relationship between the sole Ishvara and its multiple manifestations is to examine the Trimurti. Hindus believe that the three deities making up that sacred trinity—Brahma, Vishnu, and Shiva—are all expressions, or different sides of the sole universal god. It is thought that recognizing and worshipping those different aspects of God makes

26

Three deities—Brahma, Vishnu, and Shiva—make up the sacred trinity known in the Hindu faith as the Trimurti. The Trimurti (pictured) is viewed as a manifestation of the one all-powerful God.

BRAHMA

VISHNU

SHIVA

The Trimurti or Hindu Trinity.

this mysterious, otherwise unknowable Oneness more relatable to humans. As noted Hinduism expert Irina Gajjar explains,

> God, as manifested in the trinity possesses distinct, visible, tangible, depictable attributes. He has human emotions combined with God power. Brahma, Vishnu, and Shiva and their [fellow deities] engage in human activities that make them the subject of legends and that endear them to all Hindus, irrespective of their opinion of the universe or their perception of God.[20]

Core Beliefs Surrounding the Trimurti

One reason why the members of the Trimurti are so widely beloved among Hindus everywhere is because these beings and their roles and powers lie at the very heart of the Hindu belief system. "The Godhead, the three-faced holy trinity," Gajjar writes,

Some non-Hindus find the relationship between the universal God and the multiple deities that Hindus worship confusing or even disrespectful. Christians, for instance, have sometimes viewed the statues of separate Hindu gods as idols and have criticized their worship as idolatry, which the Christian God forbids. But as scholar of Hinduism Steven J. Rosen explains, idolatry "is an outsider's term for the symbols and visual images of a culture that is foreign to them." To foster a better understanding of this key Hindu religious concept, Rosen provides the following helpful analogy:

> We may find some mailboxes on the street, and if we post our letters in those boxes, they will naturally go to their destinations without difficulty. But any old box, or an imitation that we may find somewhere but that is not authorized by the post office, will not do the work. Similarly, God has an authorized representation in the Deity form, which is called *archa-vigraha*. This *archa-vigraha* is an incarnation of the supreme Lord. God will accept service through that form. The Lord is omnipotent [and] all-powerful; therefore, by his incarnation as *archa-vigraha* He can accept the service of the devotee [worshipper], just to make it convenient for the [average person].

Steven J. Rosen, *Essential Hinduism*. New York: Praeger, 2006, pp. 192–93.

"represents the idea that god's powers are infinite and that they embody and transcend [go beyond] the universe itself." Moreover, the classic stories associated with the three deities making up the Godhead define the faith's core beliefs and carry them from one generation to another. Those legends, Gajjar continues, "discuss creation and destruction. They speak of God's manifestations and God's power. They bring laughter and tears and they thrill, frighten, comfort, and teach generation after generation of Hindus. [Those] ancient stories told and retold never lose their fascination. They weave themselves into the fabric of Hindu life."[21]

Among these fundamental beliefs is that in the distant past Brahma—making up one-third of the divine trinity—created Earth and all the living things that inhabit it. Also, his consort, or divine partner, Saraswati, serves as the goddess of knowledge, and without her efforts people could not learn about themselves and the universe. Another belief is that ever since completing his duties as creator, Brahma has spent almost all of his time reciting the contents of the four Vedas over and over again. This is meant to make it clear to humanity that the basic spiritual beliefs set forth in those ancient texts are also the basis of all existence.

The first belief associated with the second member of the trinity, Vishnu, is that he long ago promised to protect the world and humanity by returning as needed in troubled times and ensuring that good triumphs over evil. Up to the present day, Hindus believe, he has been incarnated, or taken the form of an avatar, nine times. Among these guises were Narasimha, Parasurama, Vamana, Rama, and Krishna. The last two are especially renowned for their heroic antics in the two great Hindu epics, the Ramayana and the Mahabharata. Hindus believe that Vishnu will always send an avatar to aid humanity when the need arises.

> *"God's powers are infinite and . . . they embody and transcend the universe itself."*[21]
>
> —Scholar Irina Gajjar

Devotion to Vishnu is particularly strong among members of a sect, or denomination, of Hinduism called Vaishnavism. They view Vishnu as the most gifted and important of God's manifestations. Sacred to the sect are the deity's symbols, or special objects. They include the conch shell, the discus, the lotus flower, and the eagle.

Hindus further believe that the Trimurti's third member, Shiva, demolishes the world's and humanity's imperfections to clear the way for beneficial change. Thus, Shiva's acts of destruction are not hurtful or meaningless but rather ultimately constructive. The god's most dedicated followers make up a Hindu sect called Shaivism. Its artists (along with other Hindu artists) traditionally depict Shiva with a third eye, which symbolizes his wisdom, insight, and huge reserves of unbounded energy. In addition, Hindus believe that Shiva is the greatest dancer in history; supposedly in the far future, when Brahman deems the time is right, the side of his personality called Shiva will perform the so-called dance of death, which will wipe the present universe from existence.

Other Gods and Goddesses

The many other Hindu gods and goddesses play their various roles in the faith's highly complex vision of nature and the world. In some cases, these deities personify certain basic and essential aspects of life. Annapurna, Shiva's wife, for example, is the goddess of food and cooking. The belief is that she can supply food to virtually unlimited numbers of people, so Hindus request her aid when famine threatens. In a similar context, Hindu art frequently depicts Shiva asking his wife to provide him with the food items he requires to create the energy that keeps his body functioning. Many modern Hindus place images of Annapurna in their kitchens, believing this will create an abundance of plentiful and tasty foods.

Another divine figure admired by most Hindus is Dhanwantari, the gods' personal physician and, in that role, a kind of a "father of medicine" figure for humanity. Hindu artists often depict him holding a cup or bowl of life-giving medicine. At one point, according to Hindu mythology, Dhanwantari was born on Earth as the ruler of an Indian kingdom. In that role he brought the fundamental concepts of medical science to human society.

Other Hindu gods are manifestations or symbols of natural forces or powers that keep the universe functioning and in balance. Shakti, for instance, is believed to be a female force inherent in the very structure of the cosmos. She funnels energy to the various other divine beings, which makes her a kind of mother goddess, one of several in the Hindu belief system. Another mother goddess, Durga, is famous for fighting off demons that are thought to periodically threaten the other deities.

Hindu gods often incarnate on Earth as avatars. Among Vishnu's several avatars, for instance, was not only Krishna himself but also Krishna's brother, Balrama. The latter came to symbolize the ideal brother, son, or husband, who should be honest, dutiful, and

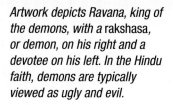
Artwork depicts Ravana, king of the demons, with a rakshasa, or demon, on his right and a devotee on his left. In the Hindu faith, demons are typically viewed as ugly and evil.

physically strong and reassuring to the family unit. In Hindu mythology Balrama accompanied Krishna on some of his adventures.

It is vital to recall that these and the numerous other Hindu gods were in ancient times, and today still are, not conceived to be separate entities unto themselves, as in true polytheistic faiths. Rather, they are diverse aspects of the lofty, distant, and mysterious one true God. When people set apart and worship the assorted sides of his personality, he becomes at least to some degree comprehensible.

Over the years a number of books, articles, and Internet sites have pointed out some close similarities between certain Hindu beliefs and certain Christian beliefs. An obvious one is that both faiths feature a trinity—three persons or aspects of the one God. Some of the other parallels between the two religions center on the characters and lives of Hinduism's Krishna and Christianity's Jesus of Nazareth. For example, in the traditions of those faiths both Krishna and Jesus were divine beings who appeared on Earth in human form. Both characters' earthly fathers were carpenters. Moreover, Krishna's mother, Devaki, was a virgin, as was Jesus's mother, Mary. Furthermore, an angel told Devaki that she was favored among women, and an angel told Mary the same thing. The parallels continue as both Jesus and Krishna were visited at birth by three so-called wise men who were guided by a star. In both cases an angel warned that the local ruler wanted to kill the infant; to escape that fate, both Krishna's and Jesus's parents fled into a wilderness area. Jesus and Krishna both performed miracles, including healing lepers and raising the dead. In still another even more striking parallel, both characters were crucified and resurrected, and then ascended back into heaven. Some Hindu writers claim that these similarities are the result of ancient Christians borrowing parts of Krishna's story; some Christian commentators say the opposite—that various ancient Hindus borrowed aspects of Jesus's story. Still other observers suggest that the similarities are merely coincidence.

Multiple Lives and Moral Consequences

These divine aspects, avatars, and/or symbols of God were in early Hindu times called *devas*. Today the term *deva* is still sometimes used that way; for example, Hindu writers occasionally refer to the three members of the Trimurti as higher devas. But more often to modern Hindus, a deva is a minor deity, usually one who oversees or controls natural forces such as wind, fire, thunder, and so forth. Devas can also be thought of as celestial beings similar to angels in the Christian religion.

Many Hindus also believe in the existence of demons, called *rakshasas,* or sometimes *asuras*. Hindu demons are similar to Christian ones, as both versions are typically viewed as physically ugly and evil. Unlike the Hindu gods, however, the Hindu demons are not aspects of God; instead, they are mortal beings who, although they possess the power to hurt and corrupt people, can also be killed. (In contrast, the gods are immortal.) Hindus describe the creation of demons in diverse ways. One of the more popular versions is that of a human who lives a particularly dishonest, violent, and worthless life and, as a punishment, is transformed into a demon after he or she dies.

According to Hindu belief, the reason a person undergoes such a conversion, or any transformation following death, is due to samsara, which translates into English as "cyclical or ever-changing world." Such a world is the basis for the Hindu belief in reincarnation. The crux of this concept is that the human soul, or atman, does not disintegrate with the body after death. Instead, the soul is repeatedly reborn in order to evolve and eventually achieve release from this unending cycle of lives by becoming one with the universal spirit—Brahman. According to one expert observer, "The atman is eternal, perfect and indestructible. The atman is born into one physical body, and when that body dies it is reborn into another body."[22] During this cycle of continuous death and rebirth, the atman enters different bodies, which can be either human or animal in form.

Meanwhile, the circumstances and experiences of each successive lifetime, or incarnation, significantly depend on a merciless law of moral consequences known as karma. Within the limitations of karma, a person's actions in one lifetime will in certain ways determine how he or she must live in the next lifetime. If one is immoral and/or cruel in the present life, she or he will undergo retribution in the following life; more often than not, that payback takes the form of a demotion in the quality of one's next incarnation. As explained on the widely respected educational website Religious Tolerance,

Through pure acts, thoughts, and devotion, one can be reborn at a higher level. Eventually, one can escape samsara and achieve enlightenment. Bad deeds can cause a person to be reborn at a lower level, or even as an animal. The unequal distribution of wealth, prestige, health, disability, suffering, etc. are thus seen as natural consequences for one's previous acts, both in this life and in previous lives.[23]

The Four Aims

Hindus believe that a person can try to keep his or her atman on the right course toward ultimate release from samsara by following the Purusarthas, a term that translates as the "Four Aims" or "Four Goals" of a good life. In Sanskrit, they are *artha*, *kama*, *dharma*, and *moksha*. Artha consists of striving for financial, managerial, or other types of material success in life. According to University of Wyoming professor Paul Flesher, "This means it is religiously important to be a successful businessman, to sell a lot of carpets for instance, or to manage a successful restaurant. It also means that it is religiously good to serve on the city council, to be active in civic organizations, or even to become a politician."[24]

> *"It is religiously good to serve on the city council, to be active in civic organizations."*[24]
>
> —University of Wyoming professor Paul Flesher

The second of the Four Aims, kama, is best understood as enjoying the pleasures that life has to offer. These can take many forms. Only a brief list of them includes creating or looking at paintings, sculptures, and other kinds of art; composing or listening to music; writing or reading poetry, novels, and other forms of literature; taking part in or watching stage plays, films, ballets, concerts, and so forth; and enjoying sex.

In the Hindu belief system such appreciation and pursuit of life's pleasures should never be taken to the extreme. Instead, enjoying the good things in life should always be accomplished within the confines of the third of the Four Aims—dharma. Not only is there no exact English translation of the word *dharma*, the concept itself has no viable equivalent in Western culture. As scholar Steven J. Rosen explains, dharma can mean a number of different things:

> In common parlance it means "right way of living," "Divine Law," "path of righteousness," "faith," and "duty." Ultimately, Dharma is the central organizing principle of the cosmos. It is that which supports and maintains all exis-

tence. Dharma is the inner reality that makes a thing what it is. It is the Dharma of the bee to make honey, of the cow to give milk, of the sun to shine, and the river to flow. It is a thing's essence.[25]

Throughout these and the other definitions for dharma, one underlying premise or principle holds true. It is hard to express it in words, but one way of describing it would be a virtuous quality inherent in existence itself—in a sense, the attribute of innate, or inborn, goodness. No one knows where it came from. God may have put it in place. Or perhaps it developed in some mysterious way on its own.

One of the Four Aims of Hindu life is to strive for financial, managerial, or other material success in life. Owning or managing a successful restaurant is an example of fulfilling this goal.

In whatever manner that dharma came to be, it gives positive meaning to both the universe and human life. Devout Hindus believe that dharma is not only important and valuable in and of itself, but also as a key qualifier or support system for both artha and kama. That is, kama and artha do not work well, and can be unproductive or even harmful, if people do not pursue the dictates of dharma along with them.

Some Hindu writers, scholars, and thinkers worry that increasing numbers of Hindus are not mindful of that reality. They think that some sectors of the global Hindu community sometimes blindly imitate Western societies, especially Britain and the United States. Rajesh Patel, the influential editor of *Hindu Voice UK* magazine, for instance, believes that a majority of Westerners tend to pursue the clearly material benefits of kama and artha without tempering them with the moral values inherent in dharma. He cites the example of the global environmental problems that humanity currently faces. "Economic gain without a sense of the necessity of maintaining the cosmic order," he writes, "is what has led to the world's environmental crisis. Life without a concept of Dharma has not created any lasting sense of happiness." He adds,

> On an individual level, pursuing Kama and Artha alone can never truly lead to a feeling of lasting satisfaction, because it is their nature to multiply their desire the more they are indulged in. Yet when permeated [saturated] with the idea of Dharma, their pursuit is transformed into something noble, beautiful and of a more enduring value. [We humans] need to rediscover our understanding of Dharma on multiple levels (individual, social, national) and what it means to live by Dharma.[26]

Thus, to take pleasure in the good things in life always within the dharma is to enjoy them in moderation. In addition, adhering to dharma is constructive and will never harm any living thing.

Ultimate Liberation

Living virtuously according to dharma, Hindus believe, is also important because doing so can reduce the number of incarnations the soul must endure. No Hindu wants that process to continue any longer than is necessary. Indeed, in the Hindu belief system those who misbehave in life in one way or another might endure many, possibly even endless, rebirths. But Hindus believe that an atman that improves itself in each successive lifetime will eventually reach a point at which no further reincarnation is necessary. This is to achieve the fourth and last of the Four Aims—moksha, or release from samsara, the cycle of rebirth and multiple lives. Devout Hindus believe that this liberation of the atman will allow it to merge with God and at last be able to contemplate all the mysteries of nature and the universe.

The degree to which most Hindus take seriously their beliefs about the Four Aims and try to apply them in everyday life cannot be overstated. They recognize that they will not manage to achieve true happiness unless they at least make a credible attempt to implement those beliefs. Patel summarizes it, saying that when classical Hinduism emerged,

> the pursuing of wealth and pleasure were given their place in the scheme of life. But these impulses were not allowed to become primary motive forces for society or to go out of control. . . . The efforts towards fulfilling Kama and Artha were placed in the context of Dharma and were therefore made noble. Hindus recognized that a life governed excessively by self-will, passion, sense-attraction, self-interest, and desire cannot be the natural whole of human existence. It cannot lead to lasting happiness.[27]

To implement these beliefs and thereby eventually achieve happiness, Hindus turn to a series of rituals and practices that are both numerous and culturally rich.

CHAPTER THREE

How Do Hindus Practice Their Faith?

Hinduism features a wide array of often elaborate, almost always colorful rituals and ceremonies intended to praise and give thanks to the sole God—the Ishvara. Based on traditions going back many centuries, these practices are most often couched in the worship, called *puja*, of God's various personifications and their avatars. For instance, when people give thanks to the preserver god Vishnu, the elephant-headed god Ganesh, or some other deity, that puja is actually aimed at the sole God.

Modern Hindus therefore take part in all sorts of pujas. Although individual rituals vary from region to region and from one divine being to another, all share some basic similarities. There is nearly always some sort of sacrifice, or offering, to the deity, for example. Also, images of the gods—called *murtis*—including statues, figurines, and paintings, are typically displayed. In addition, mantras, or prayers, are common in most Hindu ceremonies, which are performed in all venues of daily life. According to Irina Gajjar,

> Today pujas remain an important center of Hindu life. They are festive events where God is respectfully given offerings of sweetmeats, fruits, flowers, and incense. At large ceremonies, participants and visitors dressed in their finest clothes and adorned with jewelry come to homes and temples in happy moods. Most attendees enjoy worshiping with their friends and family and then sharing the treats that follow. [Religious] ceremonies, whether elaborate or simple, belong to Hinduism's living and growing memory. Longstanding cultural practices that link the present to the past become tradition.[28]

Home Worship

Gajjar's mention of people worshipping in both homes and temples is a crucial point. Hindus sometimes worship communally in temples, but more often Hindu ceremonies are held in individual homes. In part this is because Hindu worship is primarily an individual act rather than a group one. Also, and very importantly, formal Hindu ceremonies and other aspects of worship are completely voluntary; in Hinduism, a person who chooses to refrain from overt acts of worship is still seen as a good person and is not penalized by God. Thus, there are no set rules surrounding Hindu worship, only traditions that one can decide to follow or not follow.

One result of these individual and voluntary qualities of Hinduism is that home-based worship has developed into a sometimes very involved and highly structured undertaking. Most Hindus have at least a small shrine permanently set up on a table, desk, or mantle, and some homes have an entire room devoted to worship activities. The ceremonies often take place once or twice a day, although some families choose to worship a couple of times a week. "Overall, the most important part" of such worship,

> *"The most important part [of Hindu worship] is glorification, that is, the family gathers in their deity room and sings praises to God."[29]*
>
> —Scholar Steven J. Rosen

Steven J. Rosen writes, "is glorification, that is, the family gathers in their deity room and sings praises to God. In addition, the deity is offered various items in sacrifice, such as food, candles, incense, flowers, and so on. After the deity 'enjoys' these offerings, remnants are left for the worshiper and his family and friends."[29]

That sharing of offerings among the deity and worshippers resembles the sacrifices performed in ancient Greece and Rome, in which people sacrificed an animal on a burning hearth. The smoke that arose was thought to nourish the god, and the worshippers cut up and ate the meat. In Hindu sacrifices, similarly, people offer some food, and the deity is thought to partake of the invisible essence of the food, after which the worshippers eat it.

Hindu faithful surround a statue of the mother goddess Durga during a religious festival. Such festivals are an important part of Hindu life.

Over time, Hindus who worship at home collect various ceremonial items, or paraphernalia, to use in their regular rituals. One of the most common is a ghee lamp, an old-fashioned device that burns either oil or clarified butter (called ghee). According to ancient tradition, such a lamp symbolizes God leading humans from darkness into light and is also thought to promote peace on earth. Many Hindus recite a version of the following prayer while lighting the lamp: "O Deity, you are of the form of Brahman, the absolute truth. You are full of radiance. You never wither. Please bestow on me health."[30] Other typical worship paraphernalia include statues or paintings of the deity; sticks of incense that, when burned, symbolize the worshipper clearing his or her mind of all but good thoughts; a conch shell in which to pour pure water that will be offered to the deity; and food items and/or flowers to offer.

Temple Worship

In addition to burning oil and incense and making sacrificial offerings to the chosen deity, home worshippers usually chant the deity's name over and over. Such repeated recitations, like prayers, are called mantras. All of these same rituals, along with the traditional paraphernalia, are features of communal temple worship as well. In fact, Hindu temple worship is quite similar to the home-centered kind except that the communal version is on a larger scale. Moreover, most of the rituals enacted in a temple are performed by an experienced priest called a *pujari*.

> *"You are full of radiance. You never wither."[30]*
>
> —From a Hindu prayer to God

Because a Hindu temple is a large structure that has been built and decorated by the overall community, both its physical attributes and elements of worship are more elaborate than home versions. For example, the shrine, or altar, is massive and richly decorated. There is typically an imposing icon, or realistic-looking statue, of the deity to whom the temple was dedicated. Also, overall the building is decorated with multiple statues of other deities, along with other kinds of sculptures and often beautifully executed paintings of incidents from the traditional stories about those divine beings.

Among the intricate elements of temple worship are the playing of drums and other musical instruments and altering the central icon in diverse ways deemed appropriate by long-standing tradition. In a Hindu temple, Gavin Flood explains,

> puja usually comprises a rite of bathing the icon, during which various substances are rubbed on the deity's "body," such as sesame seed oil and curd [a solid dairy product made from milk]. The deity is then dressed and decorated in new clothes [and] adorned with gold, jewels, and perfumes, often receiving a dot of red turmeric on the forehead or bridge of the nose. Plates of boiled rice and sweets are offered to the deity to the accompaniment of the ringing of bells.[31]

The sacred icon is not the only one who receives the red dot on the forehead. Worshippers can also obtain that adornment, called a *bindi* or *tikka*, that they can choose to wear all the time or only on special occasions. According to Irina Gajjar, the red material is "a powder made of dried turmeric mixed with lime, that turns deep red. Mixed with water, the powder becomes a paste. The priest applies it with his fingertip, so it is round."[32] (A person can replace a *bindi* after it washes off; it does not have to be applied by a priest each and every time.) The symbolic meaning of the tikka is a third eye that is believed to produce a sort of spiritual vision that allows a person to look at his or her own inner self.

Depending on where a Hindu chooses to worship—at home, in a temple, or somewhere else—the rituals are broadly divided into three basic types. One, known as Nitya, consists of more or less daily small-scale offerings and prayers performed in the home or a local setting. A second kind of ritual—Naimittika—happens less frequently, usually in a temple, at certain times of the year. It features holiday-like festivals, including one similar to the celebration of Thanksgiving.

Pilgrimage: A Transforming Experience

The third category of worship, Kamya, consists of rituals performed in special places and is most often associated with pilgrimages. "Pilgrimage is integral to Hinduism," Flood points out. "A pilgrimage is a *tirtha yatra*, a journey to a holy place, referred to as a 'ford' (tirtha), a place for 'crossing over,' where the divine world touches or meets the human world. The tirtha is a place where the transcendent [heavenly] comes to earth, where the higher realm meets the lower, and the sacred meets the everyday.[33]

Pilgrimages to such special spots are highly encouraged among Hindus of all walks of life. Believers agree that it can be a transforming experience because visiting a unique temple or a sacred river

> *"A [Hindu] pilgrimage is a . . . journey to a holy place . . . where the divine world touches or meets the human world."[33]*
>
> —University of Wales scholar Gavin Flood

K.V. Venugopalan, an Indian writer and practicing Hindu, compiled this list of what he calls the "valuable services to society" that worshipping in a Hindu temple provides the faithful:

1. Tranquility: The temple atmosphere with its soothing vibrations of holy chants and the sanctifying presence of the Deity serves as a tranquil retreat center. It offers essential refreshing breaks that empower people to face the stresses of life.

2. Education: The temple serves as a center for higher spiritual education wherein people learn principles and practices for leading a life of moral and spiritual integrity. This education in foundational values enables people to use all their other education for socially beneficial purposes.

3. Medication: The temple acts like a hospital for the mind. The medication it provides heals the diseased mentality that impels people to addiction and criminality, both of which cause an enormous drain on the national economy.

4. Purification: The temple purifies the hearts of those who visit it regularly. This purification inspires talented people with leadership potential to blossom into pure-hearted, selfless, principle-centered leaders.

5. Love: The temple offers us a glimpse of the kingdom of God, where we are all together as family members in God's family. In a vibrant temple, people learn to form relationships at the spiritual level. This leads to the experience of a profound God-centered love that provides them deep satisfaction and dramatically improves their relationships.

K.V. Venugopalan, "Hindu Temple Visits: Things to Know, Rituals & Meanings," Temple Purohit, September 16, 2017. www.templepurohit.com.

or some other singular place is said to have a purifying effect. That is, the pilgrims believe they come closer than usual to God, and that imparts feelings of virtue, contentment, and stability.

Among the many pilgrimage sites in India, one of the more popular is the city of Varanasi (also known as Benares), which is located along the Ganges River in the country's northern sector. Since ancient times it has been identified as the hometown of the god Shiva. People come from long distances to walk down a set of stone stairs that lead right into the river. There, pilgrims eagerly bathe in the sacred waters, which are believed to have a cleansing effect. Varanasi is also a major cremation site. Each year large numbers of Hindus opt to have their ashes scattered on the Ganges in that holy city.

Also hugely popular is the Kumbha Mela festival or fair. It is held approximately once every three years in one of four places in India in rotation, so that each of the four locations becomes the festival's focus every twelve years. Each location is along a river, where the pilgrims bathe, in some cases in the nude. The crowds that gather for this event have been growing in recent decades to phenomenal sizes. An estimated 120 million pilgrims took part in the Kumbha Mela in 2013, prompting the United Nations Educational, Scientific, and Cultural Organization to call it "the largest peaceful congregation of pilgrims on earth."[34]

Common Hindu Festivals

Although Hindus view pilgrimages as particularly satisfying, they are not regular occurrences. More frequent and habitual among the faith's special rituals are religious festivals, some of which are celebrated as national holidays in India. The dates for most of these celebrations change slightly in each successive year. This is because, as Rosen explains, "Hinduism bases its reckoning of time on a lunar calendar." He goes on,

> The Indian lunar year consists of 12 months, with an intercalary [extra] month inserted once every 3 years or so, which helps the Hindu calendar approximate solar dating standards. [Although] the exact procedure of calculating such dates is somewhat complex, especially when compared with the Western [solar dating] system, Hindus engage experienced astrologers and astronomers whose special task is to assess the auspicious [favorable] time periods associated with a given festival.[35]

Many of the rituals associated with Hindu festivals are partly based on stories from Hindu mythology. Diwali, the Festival of the Lights, for example, celebrates the triumph of good over evil. Although worshippers see this in the general sense—that is, good must always defeat evil—the festival also celebrates what Hindus view as the original examples of the triumph of good. One was the killing of the hideous demon Narakaasura by Vishnu's heroic avatar Krishna. In the tale, Narakaasura rules a section of northern India near Nepal and imposes a reign of terror on the locals. The corrupt being also abducts and abuses thousands of the daughters of various minor gods. Those deities beg Krishna to intervene, which he does. In a furious battle that causes the ground to quake, he slays the demon and liberates the captive girls.

Diwali also celebrates the defeat of another horrifying demon, Ravana, by a different avatar of Vishnu—Rama. In the story, the repellent Ravana, who has ten heads and ten arms, rules what is now the island nation of Sri Lanka, located off India's southern coast. He kidnaps Rama's wife, Sita. Hurrying to Sri Lanka, Rama engages Ravana in a battle fought from chariots that fly up into the sky. After Ravana hurls thousands of flaming arrows to no effect, Rama overpowers and kills him; the demon's body then hurtles down to the ground. Shortly afterward, Rama and his wife are reunited.

Thus, the Maka Sankranti festival always occurs in January, but the exact day that the faithful observe it fluctuates from one year to the next. The name of this festival means "Entry into Capricorn," a reference to the sun passing through the constellation of Capricorn, the goat. Going far back into India's history to the time when the vast majority of people worked on farms, it marks the end of the annual harvest. Worshippers give thanks to God through sacrifice and prayer, followed by fireworks displays and sharing pastries, candy, and other sweet treats.

Another yearly festival, Shivaratri, is held in late February or early March. Hinduism's principal celebration and expression of thanks to Shiva, it consists of offerings to that deity and the singing of hymns. In a similar fashion, worshippers give thanks to Vishnu by celebrating his avatar Rama in the Ramn Navmi festival, which is held in April. In addition to enacting traditional aspects of worship, believers across India stage home-based or public readings from the Ramayana, in which Rama is the central character. There is also a festival to honor another of Vishnu's incarnations, Krishna—the Krishna Janamashtami, which is celebrated in late August or early September.

Although these and the several other religious festivals that Hindus observe are seen as important, all pale in significance to the biggest sacred holiday of the year—the Diwali (or Divali or Deepavali). Held in late October or early November, it is also commonly referred to as the Festival of the Lights. The word *lights*

Small earthenware oil lamps are set out during the holiday known as Diwali. The lamps are intended to help the goddess Lakshmi find her way to worshippers so that she can bestow good fortune on them.

here refers partly to traditional fireworks displays staged multiple times during the five-day-long celebration. But the main reference to lights in the festival's name derives from the widespread custom of decorating houses, shops, and public places with small earthenware oil lamps. People usually place them in rows in windows and doorways. This practice is based on the legend that the lights will help Lakshmi, goddess of wealth, find her way to worshippers so she can bestow good fortune on them. Gajjar writes,

> *"Hindus ask [the goddess] Lakshmi [to] bless their account books so that their businesses and finances may flourish."*[36]
>
> —Scholar Irina Gajjar

A few days before Diwali, people decorate their homes with new or fresh furnishings and with flowers and leaves. The most talented family members make a big colorful design called a *rangoli* at the entrance, using grains [including wheat] and rice. [Also] sweets are prepared for guests who will come to call. [Often] Hindus ask Lakshmi [to] bless their account books so that their businesses and finances may flourish. [Meanwhile, most] families hold a puja in their homes to pay their respects to God, Lakshmi, and to their elders.[36]

Celebrating Childhood Rituals

The practice of the Hindu faith also includes the *sanskara*, a collection of rituals connected to important milestones, or rites of passage, in people's lives. These include ceremonies for both children and adults. The childhood rituals include some performed while a mother is pregnant, with the aim of protecting the fetus from harm; an observance of the cutting of the umbilical cord shortly after birth; a celebration of the baby's first glimpse of the sun; the first shaving of a child's head—called the Mundan—usually held before age three; for boys, an observation of their first facial shaving; and for girls, a ceremony to mark their initial menstruation, seen as the beginning of young womanhood.

Yoga is one of the oldest practices in the Hindu religion and references to it can be found in various ancient Hindu writings, among them the *Yoga Sutras of Patanjali*, the *Bhagavad Gita*, and the *Hatha Yoga Pradipika*. As a spiritual ritual in the faith, yoga is viewed as one of the several ways that a person can strive for enlightenment, or a mental state in which he or she is closer to God. The person accomplishes this by doing a number of accepted traditional physical postures and exercises on a regular basis. By doing so, he or she can hopefully gain as much mastery as possible over his or her own body, mind, and emotions. The belief is that over time that individual, called a yogi, will gradually acquire knowledge about the nature of reality, which Hindus think is far from obvious to the average person. In turn, when the yogi does become familiar with reality, he or she can potentially experience a sort of union with God (Brahman) or one of the many lesser deities that Hindus view as manifestations of God.

In the United States and most other Western countries, many non-Hindus practice the exercises associated with yoga without attempting to achieve the specific spiritual aspects that Hindus typically pursue. For the Christian, Jew, Muslim, or nonbeliever who practices yoga daily or weekly, the aims tend to be improved health, mental clarity, and emotional well-being.

Of the sanskara performed early in life, one that all Hindus see as particularly important is the name-giving ceremony, called the Namkaran. Numerous experts on Hindu culture in India and elsewhere have written articles, pamphlets, and even books containing guidelines for naming children. They all stress that it is vital to choose a name that has some sort of positive meaning, one that the child will be proud of when he or she grows up. One guide advises choosing names such as Virsen, which means a victor on the battlefield, or Vedvrata, meaning someone who studies the sacred Vedas. Other experts propose different naming guidelines, among them ones associated with the heavenly bodies or the months in which children are born. In addition, most guides strongly urge parents to pick names that can be pronounced fairly easily.

Whichever name is chosen, a majority of Hindus follow certain rituals during the Namkaran. Both parents, along with invited guests, should be present, and when possible a local priest should be involved. According to Indian researcher Subhamoy Das,

> The priest performs the ritual with prayers to the gods, to Agni, the god of fire, to the elements, and to the spirits of the ancestors. Rice grains are spread on a bronze dish and the father writes the chosen name on it using a gold stick while chanting [Agni's] name. Then he whispers the name into the child's right ear, repeating it four times along with a prayer. All others present now repeat a few words after the priest to formally accept the name. This is followed by the blessings of the elders along with gifts and ends with a feast with family and friends. Usually, the family astrologer also presents the child's horoscope at this ceremony.[37]

Not long after the naming ceremony it is time for another early childhood ritual, the Annaprasana, which celebrates a child's first feeding of solid food. For many centuries it was performed only for boys, in part because male children were long favored over female ones. In modern times, however, the Annaprasana began to be held for girls too. The traditional Indian foods used most often for this ceremony are rice, lentils, and ghee.

Another popular sanskara, the Karnavedha, observes a milestone that typically occurs during a child's third or fifth year; namely, the first ear piercing. Up until the twentieth century, both boys and girls participated in equal measure. But eventually fewer and fewer young males wanted to take part, arguing that getting their ears pierced might make them look too feminine and leaving them open to ridicule by other boys. As a result, today the Karnavedha is performed primarily for young girls.

Still another childhood ritual, the Vidyarambha, celebrates the start of a child's education. In centuries past, when young Indian children did not attend formal schools, the ceremony usually took place at home. Sometimes with a parent's help, the child traced the letters of a short prayer either in sand or in a layer of rice grains spread across a tray. The prayer was directed to a deity, most often Saraswati, one of whose roles was goddess of knowledge. Today the Vidyarambha is more often performed on a child's first day at school, where he or she learns to write the alphabet.

Wedding and Funeral Rites

Of the adult-oriented sanskara, wedding rituals tend to be the longest—lasting several days—and the most expensive, colorful, and dramatic. There are several prewedding ceremonies, including pujas intended to call on various deities to impart positive energies to the marriage, the decoration of the bride's hands and feet with intricate henna patterns by her girlfriends, and songs and dances staged by the bride's family to entertain the groom's family and friends. The actual wedding ceremony often costs enormous sums, and it is common for families to go heavily into debt to pay for it.

On the day of the actual ceremony, the bride and groom, as well as their guests, wear magnificent costumes, frequently studded with real jewels. Whenever possible, the groom arrives in a dramatic manner, for instance riding a horse, chariot, or elephant. "The actual moment of marriage," Gajjar says, "occurs when the bride and groom, hand in hand and in the presence of witnesses, take seven steps around the sacred fire."[38]

Hindu funeral rites, called Antyeshti, can also be quite involved, although they are not nearly as expensive as wedding ceremonies. Although most Hindus think they will be reincarnated, a person's death is still seen as a sad occurrence. This is especially true if the person is very young when he or she dies. It is also common for older Hindus, who may assume they will be dying in the near future, to feel apprehensive or anxious. There may be a feeling of certainty that he or she will be reborn following the departure from the current life. Yet the person does not know how many times she or he will be reincarnated; nor can that individual guess what each of those later lives will be like.

Actual funeral rites vary somewhat from place to place. But it is very common for family and friends to gather together briefly out of respect for the dead person's life and passing. The vast

A young couple in Bali takes part in a traditional Hindu wedding ceremony. In such ceremonies, the bride and groom and even wedding guests often wear magnificent, jewel-studded clothing.

majority of Hindus practice cremation. That approach is based on the Vedic teaching that the incinerated corpse becomes a sacrifice to the fire god, Agni. It is thought that Agni then proceeds to share that offering with other deities. Also, God ensures that the atoms and molecules that made up the person's body will, through the sacrifice, return to nature, where they will be recycled in the bodies of generations to come.

The time and place of a cremation are often viewed as crucial. Most Hindus prefer, if possible, to have their cremated remains spread at a place of pilgrimage or in the waters of a sacred river. They hope this will help the soul find safe passage to its next incarnation. Most people, however, are not fortunate enough to have their remains disposed of in that favored manner. More often than not, after the crematorium burns the body it returns the ashes to the family, which either buries them on town lands set aside for that purpose or keeps them at home.

The rituals surrounding marriage and death are like all the other Hindu rituals in the sense that they invoke the blessings of God and seek to create happiness, or at least positive outcomes. Based on ancient traditions, they emphasize the importance of the individual and her or his needs and feelings. As Flood puts it, Hindu religious practices provide "continuity of tradition through the generations, [convey] implicit Hindu values, and set the parameters for the Hindu's sense of identity."[39]

CHAPTER FOUR

What Challenges Does Hinduism Face in the Modern World?

In Hinduism's earliest centuries, whatever challenges it faced were confined to the faith's original homeland — India — because virtually all Hindus dwelled in that geographic region. However, during Hinduism's classical and medieval periods, varying numbers of the faithful began to migrate across Southeast Asia. In this way, Hindu communities grew up in what are now Thailand, Afghanistan, Bangladesh, Vietnam, Indonesia, Malaysia, Singapore, and several neighboring lands. This was the beginning of what modern scholars dubbed the Hindu diaspora, a term referring to a given population that has been split up and scattered.

The Hindu diaspora took another major turn during the nineteenth and twentieth centuries when groups of the faithful moved to other parts of the globe. As a result of all these migrations, Hindu communities can be found in a majority of countries, although more than 90 percent of Hindus still live in India. There are about 13 million Hindus in Bangladesh, for instance, and 3.6 million in Pakistan. Roughly 2.2 million Hindus live in the United States; 800,000 in Britain; 550,000 in South Africa; 23,000 in Norway; and 6,000 in Brazil.

According to Hindu authorities in those and other nations, by far the biggest challenge that members of the faith face is discrimination and persecution. As might be expected, the degree to which they are harassed varies from country to country. The Hindu American Foundation (HAF), a widely respected and influential Hindu advocacy group, says that discrimination tends to be most serious in nine nations, most of them in southern Asia. Countries in other parts of the world, HAF points out, experience similar problems but on a smaller scale. In the 2017 edition of its annual report on violations of human rights aimed at Hindus, HAF states,

> Hindu minorities living in countries throughout South Asia and other parts of the world are subject to varying degrees of legal and institutional discrimination, restrictions on their religious freedom, social prejudice, violence, social persecution, and economic and political marginalization. Hindu women are especially vulnerable and face kidnappings and forced conversions in countries such as Bangladesh and Pakistan. In several countries where Hindus are minorities, non-state actors advance a discriminatory and exclusivist agenda, often with the tacit or explicit support of the state. Persecution by state and non-state actors alike has led a growing number of Hindus to flee their country of origin and live as refugees.[40]

Hindu Communities Are Targeted

The nations singled out in the report for their abuses of Hindus are Afghanistan, Bangladesh, Malaysia, Pakistan, Bhutan, Sri Lanka, Fiji, Saudi Arabia, and Trinidad and Tobago. According to HAF, members of the majority religions in these countries, often in concert with government authorities, consistently harass and even attack Hindus and other minorities. Typically, HAF states, the oppressors use "violent tactics to achieve their religious-political goals, including bombings, political assassinations and targeted killings, attacks on security personnel, and mass violence against minorities and atheists."[41]

The reasons for this systematic discrimination and violence vary slightly from one place to another. But overall, anti-Hindu activities in southern Asia

> "[Persecution] has led a growing number of Hindus to flee their country of origin and live as refugees."[40]
>
> —The Hindu American Foundation

Hindu women from Bangladesh protest violence directed at that country's Hindu population. Assaults, bombings, and arson prompted thousands of Hindus to flee to neighboring India.

and elsewhere in the world are consistently motivated by the same factors. They include dislike, or even outright hatred, of foreigners and immigrants; the related fear that those outsiders will dilute or pollute the majority culture; intense religious intolerance; racial prejudice; and local laws that favor the majority culture and religion and discourage or discriminate against minority cultures and faiths.

The combined effect of these factors is at times a potent and frightening campaign against the local Hindu community. In 2001 and 2002, for example, members of the Muslim majority in Bangladesh targeted the Hindu community in an unrelenting manner for more than 150 days. There were some eighteen thousand incidents that can be categorized as major crimes. They included murders of Hindus; bombings and arson against Hindu homes, businesses, and temples; rape of Hindu women; and theft of cars and other Hindu property. The anti-Hindu activity became

A particularly disturbing example of anti-Hindu discrimination took place in Karachi, Pakistan, in December 2017. Three armed men barged into a Hindu home and held the family hostage for a few hours. Then, on their way out, the intruders abducted one of the children, a fourteen-year-old girl. The distraught family later learned that the young woman was taken to an undisclosed location and was forcibly converted to Islam. Also, she was forced to marry an adult Muslim man, and local court officials said there was nothing they could do to get the girl back. According to a December 2017 report posted on the Hindu-run website Struggle for Hindu Existence,

> The family members alleged that local police, too, were not interested in re-covering the girl. [The parents] demanded that the girl should be recovered and produced before a court. [Later] the family appealed to higher Pakistani officials, who said they would investigate the incident. To date, that investigation has not produced any results, leading many Hindus to suspect that the officials do not intend to try to recover the girl.

Struggle for Hindu Existence, "Minor Hindu Girls Are Abducted, Forcibly Converted to Islam for Marriage in Pakistan," December 21, 2017. https://hinduexistence.org.

so severe that an estimated half-million Hindus fled to neighboring India, where they were labeled refugees. Similar assaults on Hindus occurred periodically in Bangladesh between 2002 and 2017.

For the most part, government authorities did little or nothing to stop these episodes of civil havoc and persecution. As HAF explains, since Bangladesh's formation during the 1970s, the nation's constitution has been repeatedly amended to make it conform more to Islamic laws and values. Along the way, most clauses that originally guaranteed religious and individual freedoms were removed and replaced by ones stressing absolute loyalty to the Islamic faith. This "preeminence given to Islam in the Constitution," HAF states, "conflicts with and weakens other provisions protecting religious freedom and equal protection [and] renders them ineffective in guaranteeing the rights of minorities. It has also institutionalized second-class citizen status of non-Muslims and empowered radical groups to violate the rights of minorities with impunity."[42]

One of many examples of such civil rights violations cited in the 2017 HAF report was the case of a fifty-five-year-old Hindu priest named Jogeshwar Roy. In February 2016, as he sat in his local temple preparing for an upcoming worship session, six Islamic militants attacked the building. They fired guns and threw grenades, all the while shouting praises to God and warning Hindus standing outside to get out of Bangladesh. Entering the temple, the intruders stabbed Roy and slit his throat, killing him. The incident was one of several similar targeted killings of Hindus in that nation in 2016.

Social and Legal Discrimination

Besides carrying out blatant violent attacks, including murder and rape, those who have persecuted Hindus in the nations cited in HAF's report have also perpetrated numerous cases of social discrimination and personal abuse. Widespread, for instance, are incidents in which Hindu children are seized and converted to Islam without the parents' consent. Most commonly seen, according to HAF, are cases in which the father is Muslim and the wife is Hindu. In a 2013 case in Pakistan, a twenty-nine-year-old Hindu woman had recently become legally separated from her Muslim husband and was raising the two children, ages five and eight, herself. One day she came home from work to find that her estranged husband had taken the children out of school without her consent. She later discovered that he had begun raising the youngsters himself and instilling in them Islamic teachings and values.

When the woman challenged these actions in the town where her husband lived, a local Muslim official told her she would have to pursue the matter in a local court. She did so, and at first the court granted custody of the children, a boy and a girl, to her husband. Desperate, she appealed the case to a higher court, which returned the children's custody to her.

However, the degree to which all levels of Pakistani society could combine to marginalize a minority woman soon became clear. Not long after the children returned to her home, her husband abducted their son. The woman intervened, trying to stop the crime. But as she did so, eyewitnesses reported, she was "dragged [by a car] along the stone-strewn road outside her house until she dropped to the ground, scratched and sobbing, as her ex-husband drove off."[43] Later, in a courageous move, the woman went to a still higher court. The court, however, awarded permanent custody of her son to her husband, although it did allow her to keep her daughter.

The HAF report and other similar studies have recorded many other examples of social and legal discrimination against Hindus in places where they make up a minority of the population. These studies suggest that the situation in Pakistan, an outspoken political enemy of India, is particularly troublesome and disturbing. According to a 2016 online article published by HAF, many of the more than 3 million Hindus

> in Pakistan are compelled to pay regular sums, as a type of ransom, to extortionists and local leaders in exchange for the physical security of their families and themselves. It is conventional wisdom that no job higher than a clerk's post may be obtained by a Hindu. Furthermore, Hindus usually need a Muslim as a silent partner in order to run a business.[44]

In addition, HAF states, numerous Hindu temples in Pakistan have been vandalized, burned down, or converted into government offices. Also common have been the theft of Hindu land parcels and the arrest and detainment of Hindus on false charges. In addition, hundreds of Hindus have been kidnapped and held for ransom.

Overt Religious Intolerance

Destroying or converting temples is clearly a form of violation of religious rights and worship. The reports issued by HAF and other watchdog groups describe many other examples of overt religious intolerance in the countries studied. In this regard, Saudi Arabia has been called a major offender. One incident described online by the news source *Asia News* tells about incidents that occurred in the Saudi city of Riyadh over the course of several years.

The Saudis maintain a force of religious police, *Asia News* explains. The officers' job is to find and shut down any places or centers of worship that are not related to Islam. This is because it is illegal in that nation to maintain a public place of worship other than a mosque. At one point, the police discovered a secret makeshift Hindu temple and closed it down. In the process, they arrested and deported three worshippers they found there.

Moreover, it is not just actual Hindu (or other non-Muslim) places of worship that are regularly targeted. It is common knowledge that Hindus everywhere often worship informally in their homes. In doing so, those who live in Saudi Arabia are not breaking the country's law against worshipping in a public venue such as a church or temple. The country is host to around

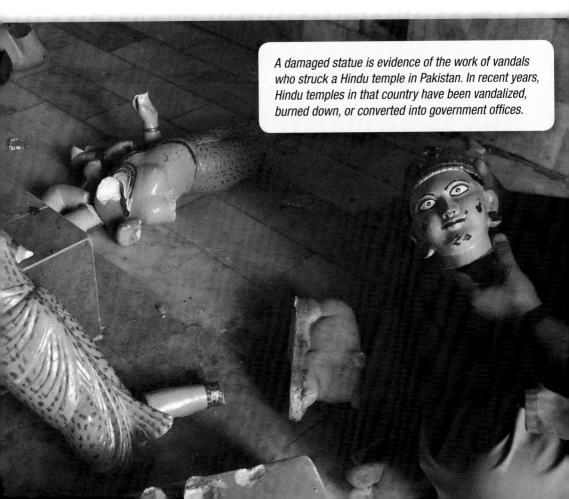

A damaged statue is evidence of the work of vandals who struck a Hindu temple in Pakistan. In recent years, Hindu temples in that country have been vandalized, burned down, or converted into government offices.

Empowering Minority Hindu Communities

For a long time, most diaspora Hindus suffering abuses by anti-Hindu elements in various nations felt so helpless and afraid that they dared not fight back and challenge their persecutors. But in recent years that situation has been steadily changing, as explained by noted Indian-born human rights advocate Samir Kalra.

> Hindu minorities in a number of countries are becoming increasingly vocal and have formed advocacy and human rights groups to assert their rights, after years of staying relatively silent out of fear. Unfortunately, in many instances, these efforts have been disjointed or not unified. We hope that these Hindus can better organize themselves and the various groups in any given country can come together on a common united platform and collectively advocate for their rights. It's also critical that Hindu organizations build relationships with other human rights groups, both domestically and internationally, to help ensure that their issues are taken up and that they have a stronger voice. Moreover, Hindu organizations that already exist need to create more programs that educate the community in their respective countries in order to empower them. . . . [Also] Indian Hindu groups can play a critical role in assisting persecuted Hindu diaspora communities. For one, they can provide direct grant assistance to local Hindu groups in affected countries by supporting education, women's empowerment, and other social programs to uplift the community, while also strengthening the capacity of local Hindus to mobilize and advocate for their rights.

Quoted in *Swarajya*, "The Discrimination Hindus Face Around the Globe and What They Can Do About It," July 2, 2017. https://swarajyamag.com.

9 million foreigners, most of whom are menial workers. To retain those workers, the government made a policy of tolerating non-Muslim religious practices as long as they are conducted privately. In theory, then, the Saudi government should allow Hindus to worship at home.

The problem is that the Saudi religious police randomly break with that policy. According to the HAF report,

> Even the private religious practice of non-Muslim workers is severely restricted. Although the Saudi government proclaimed that non-Muslims were allowed to worship in private, that right has not been clearly defined. Consequently, religious vigilantes and police have frequently harassed, assaulted, and interfered with private worship of non-Muslims. Furthermore, visitors and non-residents often complain that the police and customs authorities routinely confiscate private religious material, including books and symbols, upon entry into the country.[45]

America Is Not Immune

Saudi Arabia, Pakistan, Bangladesh, and the other countries detailed in the studies are not the only ones where anti-Hindu discrimination occurs. The United States, which has a major reputation as a beacon for religious freedom and tolerance, is not immune. It is true that US incidents of anti-Hindu discrimination are not as numerous as those in southern Asia. Yet they are nonetheless illegal and harm individuals and families.

Typical of such incidents in America is one that occurred in February 2017 in Payton, Colorado. A Hindu man—who had earlier legally immigrated to the country from India—awoke one morning to find his house covered with animal feces and racist slogans. Two weeks later, in a small Kansas town, a former member of the US Navy walked into a bar, pulled out a gun, and shot two Hindu men, killing one. According to an article in the *New Yorker* magazine, the perpetrator shouted, "Get out of my country!"[46] just before firing. He later told police that he thought the victims were Muslims from Iran.

This and similar incidents show that Hindus are attacked in the United States most often because they are mistaken for Middle Eastern Muslims. The author of the *New Yorker* article comments, "The racist's calling card is ignorance. He cannot discriminate (if that is the right word) between nationalities and religions, between Indians and Saudis and Egyptians, Hindus, and Muslims."[47]

Giving the Faith a Bad Name?

Although persecution of Hindus in various parts of the world has been a problem in recent years, to a lesser degree Hindus themselves have been accused of perpetrating inhumane acts against non-Hindus. This has been no less a burden for Hinduism than anti-Hindu attacks because bad acts committed by Hindus give the entire faith a bad name. Devout Hindus say that it is hardly fair for them to complain about unfair treatment at the hands of non-Hindus if fellow Hindus commit acts of the same kind against people who do not belong to the Hindu religion.

"The racist's calling card is ignorance. He cannot discriminate . . . between nationalities and religions."[47]

—*The New Yorker* magazine

One such case that made headlines across India, for example, occurred early in 2018 in the Indian province of Uttar Pradesh. A teenage Muslim girl was raped and named a provincial Hindu politician as her attacker. Under traditional Indian laws, a person accused of rape must be confined in jail, usually without benefit of bail, until the case goes to court. In this case, however, the accused man belonged to the Bharatiya Jarata Party (BJP), or Indian People's Party. A right-wing group, the BJP favors Indian culture over Western customs and laws. Although the accused man's exact reasoning remains unclear, he evidently felt that his spending time in jail before the trial was too much like a British or American penalty.

Whatever his thinking on the matter may have been, local magistrates allowed him to ignore the law and at least temporarily escape the consequences of the crime. He remained free to come and go as he pleased in the months before the trial. This series of events was loudly criticized by non-BJP Hindus all over India.

Considered by many Hindus to be far worse was another case that occurred in early 2018 in the northern India district of Kathua, located near the province of Kashmir. Asifa Bano, a little girl who belonged to a nomadic Muslim tribe, was grazing horses when a Hindu man approached her. He led her to a nearby Hindu temple. There, a group of eight grown Hindu men held her prisoner, drugged her, and raped her repeatedly for five days before finally killing her with a rock.

When local police took the accused men to court, dozens of Hindu lawyers appeared and tried to keep the officers away from the suspects. These lawyers argued that the men had a right to do what they did to the girl because she was a Muslim. Only when the police called for and received backup did the lawyers disperse. The police eventually found that the temple's janitor had planned the kidnapping, rape, and murder. The man actually went so far as to try to bribe the police to get them to drop the case, but to no avail.

Hindus all over India said this crime perpetrated by fellow Hindus sickened and disturbed them. They feel that so-called religious nationalists—right-wing individuals who feel that Hindus should and can be above the law—are gaining too much attention and sympathy in the country. Hindus are supposed to be humane people who uphold the law and fight for goodness, they say. As for what to do about the problem, many Hindu Indians have called for going back to old-fashioned Hindu values in all social and political situations. Indian journalist Ravi Shankar spoke for many when he wrote the following passage in a widely circulated article:

> The moment has come now to save Hinduism from fake Hindus and restore humanity to politics and society. The innocence of democracy, which believes that all are equal and justice gives all citizens a fair deal, has to be resurrected in this age of sadistic pretenders. Let the girl of meadows [Bano] not have died in vain as an unsuspecting and un-avenged martyr at the hands of savages who use an ancient religion and pervert patriotism in the name of god.[48]

Possible Remedies

Whether it is Hindus overstepping the bounds of decency and legality or non-Hindus persecuting innocent Hindus, a majority of experts say that the best remedy is information—educating people about different religions, nationalities, and racial groups. HAF strongly supports the idea of incorporating such information into school curricula. Also, it states, the teachers in those schools should receive sensitivity training regarding discriminatory attitudes toward religious minorities.

Regarding the many cases of anti-Hindu discrimination in places like Bangladesh, Saudi Arabia, and Pakistan, HAF and other organizations that investigate such incidents have published recommendations for possible solutions. In its 2017 report, for instance, HAF suggested some steps that could be taken in Pakistan. They are very similar to the proposals the group made for the other nations singled out in the report. One such proposal is for the governments of those countries to provide adequate security to Hindu temples and other buildings where residents of minority faiths worship.

Another potential solution is to pass a law that reserves a few seats for Hindus and members of other minorities in both the provincial and national legislatures. This would give individuals in minority faiths like Hinduism a voice in local politics and a legal platform for stating their grievances. HAF also recommends that the governments in question should revise or repeal existing laws related to religious and social discrimination. In addition, advocates of equitable change suggest that the nations singled out in the HAF report should

> train local law enforcement to better deal with vigilante justice and mob attacks on individuals accused of committing blasphemy. [There should also be training of] local law enforcement on how to deal with kidnappings, forced conversions, and involuntary marriages of Hindu and Christian girls. Police must also crack down on mosques that promote such activities and ensure the safety of girls and their families.[49]

HAF and other Hindu advocacy groups have also appealed to the greater international community. They have called on the United Nations (UN) to focus more attention on the poor human rights records of nations like Bangladesh, Pakistan, and Saudi Arabia. Moreover, the advocates have urged the UN to address the status of Hindus who have fled those countries. Often they do not have official refugee status, which hinders their settling in nations that treat religious minorities better. The UN should grant those stateless individuals refugee status, HAF says.

Many of the refugees make their way to India, and the decent treatment some have experienced provides hope to other mistreated members of the Hindu diaspora. In a July 2017 interview given to a leading Indian magazine, the chief author of the HAF report, Samir Kalra, said, "We've been encouraged by some positive steps that have been taken by the government towards Hindu refugee populations that have sought refuge in India." He

Hindu advocacy groups have seen signs of progress in global efforts to help Hindu refugee populations. Hindus worldwide continue to practice their faith and look to the future with hope.

added that he hoped more would be done in the future to assist Hindu refugees around the globe. Finally, Kalra promised that going forward HAF will never relent in its efforts to keep the problem of anti-Hindu abuses in the public eye. "We will continue to monitor and reach out to media outlets," he declared. The goal is "to ensure that the important issues in this report are covered and to raise awareness about the plight facing Hindu minorities."[50]

The individuals who run HAF are well aware that they have their work cut out for them. They do not expect the problem of persecution—either *against* or *by* Hindus—to disappear overnight. But they remain ever vigilant in hopes of maintaining a positive reputation for one of the world's most ancient and noble faiths.

SOURCE NOTES

Introduction: The Power of Good Deeds

1. Quoted in AumAmen, "Story of a Thief Who Became a Monk." http://aumamen.com.

2. Quoted in AumAmen, "Story of a Thief Who Became a Monk."

3. Quoted in AumAmen, "Story of a Thief Who Became a Monk."

4. Mahabharata 5:1517.

5. Matthew 7:12.

Chapter One: The Origins of Hinduism

6. Gavin Flood, *An Introduction to Hinduism*. New York: Cambridge University Press, 2006, p. 6.

7. Karel Werner, *A Popular Dictionary of Hinduism*. Chicago: NTC, 1997, p. 5.

8. Devdutt Pattanaik, "Was Harappan Civilization Vedic or Hindu?," December 15, 2016. www.dailyo.in.

9. Hillary Rodrigues, "Fire in Hinduism," Mahavidya, June 23, 2008. www.mahavidya.ca.

10. BBC, "Brahman: God of Gods?" www.bbc.co.uk.

11. Quoted in AumAmen, "Hanuman Chalisa." http://aumamen .com.

12. Jukka O. Miettinen, "India: Early Literature and Theater," *Asian Traditional Theatre & Dance*, Theatre Academy of the University of the Arts Helsinki, 2018. http://disco.teak.fi.

13. Bhagavad Gita 2:12–18, trans. Sanderson Beck. www.san .beck.org.

14. University of Missouri Museum of Art and Archaeology, "Seeing the Divine in Hindu Art." https://maa.missouri.edu.

15. Vidya Dehejia, "Hinduism and Hindu Art," *Heilbrunn Timeline of Art History*, Metropolitan Museum of Art. www.metmuseum.org.

16. Marilyn McFarlane, "Sacred Stories: Wisdom from World Religions," Authors Guild. www.authorsguild.net.

17. Mark Cartwright, "Hindu Architecture." Ancient History Encyclopedia, September 4, 2015. www.ancient.eu.

Chapter Two: What Do Hindus Believe?

18. Kim Knott, *Hinduism: A Very Short Introduction*. New York: Oxford University Press, 2016, p. xiii.

19. Kauai's Hindu Monastery, "For Facts of Hinduism." www.himalayanacademy.com.

20. Irina Gajjar, *On Hinduism*. Edinburg, VA: Axos, 2013, pp. 22–23.

21. Gajjar, *On Hinduism*, pp. 26, 72.

22. Bitesize, "Hinduism: Good and Evil," BBC. www.bbc.co.uk.

23. Religious Tolerance, "Hinduism: A General Introduction." www.religioustolerance.org.

24. Paul Flesher, "Hinduism: Living the Religious Life," Religious Studies Program, University of Wyoming. www.uwyo.edu.

25. Steven J. Rosen, *Essential Hinduism*. New York: Praeger, 2006, p. 35.

26. Rajesh Patel, "Purusharthas: The Four Great Aims of Life." https://hinduperspective.com.

27. Patel, "Purusharthas: The Four Great Aims of Life."

Chapter Three: How Do Hindus Practice Their Faith?

28. Gajjar, *On Hinduism*, pp. 109–10.

29. Rosen, *Essential Hinduism*, p. 195.

30. Quoted in Hindu Janajagruti Samiti, "Why Is a Ghee Lamp Preferred During Puja Ritual?" www.hindujagruti.org.

31. Flood, *An Introduction to Hinduism*, p. 209.

32. Gajjar, *On Hinduism*, p. 112.

33. Flood, *An Introduction to Hinduism*, p. 212.

34. United Nations Educational, Scientific, and Cultural Organization, "Kumbh Mela." https://ich.unesco.org.

35. Rosen, *Essential Hinduism*, p. 207.

36. Gajjar, *On Hinduism*, pp. 138–39.

37. Subhamoy Das, "Namkaran Is the Hindu Naming Ceremony," ThoughtCo., September 27, 2017. www.thoughtco.com.

38. Gajjar, *On Hinduism*, pp. 124–25.

39. Flood, *An Introduction to Hinduism*, p. 223.

Chapter Four: What Challenges Does Hinduism Face in the Modern World?

40. Hindu American Foundation, *Hindus in Southeast Asia and the Diaspora: A Survey of Human Rights*, 2017, p. 5. www.hafsite.org.

41. Hindu American Foundation, *Hindus in Southeast Asia and the Diaspora*, p. 36.

42. Hindu American Foundation, *Hindus in Southeast Asia and the Diaspora*, p. 35.

43. Quoted in Hindu American Foundation, *Hindus in Southeast Asia and the Diaspora*, p. 47.

44. Hindu American Foundation, "Discrimination and Persecution: The Plight of Hindus in Pakistan." www.hafsite.org.

45. Hindu American Foundation, *Hindus in Southeast Asia and the Diaspora*, p. 93.

46. Quoted in Amitava Kumar, "Being Indian in Trump's America," *New Yorker*, March 15, 2017. www.newyorker.com.

47. Kumar, "Being Indian in Trump's America."

48. Ravi Shankar, "Save Hinduism from Fake Hindus to Keep the Faith," *New Indian Express*, April 14, 2018. www.newindianexpress.com.

49. Hindu American Foundation, *Hindus in Southeast Asia and the Diaspora*, p. 62.

50. Quoted in *Swarajya*, "The Discrimination Hindus Face Around the Globe and What They Can Do About It," July 2, 2017. https://swarajyamag.com.

FOR FURTHER RESEARCH

Books

Swami Achuthananda, *Many, Many, Many Gods of Hinduism*. Hauppauge, NY: Reliance Communications, 2013.

Gavin Flood and Charles Martin, trans., *The Bhagavad Gita*. New York: W.W. Norton, 2012.

Arun L. Kumar and John Humphries, *Lord Krishna: His Life and Times*. Charleston, SC: Amazon Digital Services, 2017. Kindle.

Archia Sattar and Sonali Zohra, *Ramayana: An Illustrated Retelling*. Brooklyn, NY: Restless, 2018.

Shalu Sharma, *Hinduism for Beginners*. Charleston, SC: Amazon Digital Services, 2016. Kindle.

Muari N. Tiwary, *Essential Hinduism*. Charleston, SC: Amazon Digital Services, 2016. Kindle.

Internet Sources

Art of Living, "The Symbolism of Ganesha." www.artofliving.org /wisdom/knowledge-sheets/symbolism-ganesha.

Subhamoy Das, "10 of the Most Important Hindu Gods," ThoughtCo., March 23, 2018. www.thoughtco.com/top-hindu -deities-1770309.

Harvard Divinity School Religious Literary Project, "Karma: The Way of Action." https://rlp.hds.harvard.edu/karma-way-action.

Hindu Janajagruti Samiti, "Why Is a Ghee Lamp Preferred During Puja Ritual?" www.hindujagruti.org/hinduism/knowledge/article /why-is-ghee-lamp-preferred-to-oil-lamp-during-puja-ritual.html.

Jukka O. Miettinen, "India: Early Literature and Theater," *Asian Traditional Theatre & Dance*, Theatre Academy Helsinki, 2018. http://disco.teak.fi/asia/early-literature-and-theatre.

University of Missouri Museum of Art and Archaeology, "Seeing the Divine in Hindu Art." https://maa.missouri.edu/exhibit/hindu art.

Websites

ReligionFacts (www.religionfacts.com). Under "Hindu Rituals and Practices," this extensive site contains short overviews of the principal Hindu rituals, each with a link to an article with a much longer, more detailed account.

Religions: Hinduism (www.bbc.co.uk/religion/religions/hinduism/). This BBC website provides excellent information about the Hindu faith, including history, deities, holy days, ethics, tests, worship, and more.

Templenet (www.templenet.com). This outstanding website's "Indian Temple Architecture" web page combines informative facts and texts with beautiful photos of Hindu temples around the world.

INDEX

PICTURE CREDITS

ABOUT THE AUTHOR

Historian and award-winning author Don Nardo has written numerous books about the ancient and medieval worlds, their peoples, and their cultures, including the birth and growth of the major religions in those societies. Mr. Nardo, who also composes and arranges orchestral music, lives with his wife, Christine, in Massachusetts.